LIFE'S VAGARIES

(Fourteen Short Stories)

By ...

STEPHEN M. GILL

Vesta Publications
P. O. Box 1641
Cornwall, Ontario, K6H 5V6
Canada

April 1974

© Stephen M. Gill, 1974

ISBN 0-9690996-5-7

DEDICATED

TO

MY GOOD FRIEND—

GOPAL BHARDWAJ

ACKNOWLEDGEMENT

MY GRATEFUL THANKS TO BETTY BLUE FOR HER HELPFUL ADVICE ON THESE SHORT STORIES AND ALSO FOR READING THE FINAL PAGE PROOFS.

Made and printed in Canada

TABLE OF CONTENTS

PREFACE

In an age in which it seems the accepted thing to substitute that which is erotic or violent for true art, it is refreshing to find an author such as Stephen M. Gill.

Using a simple narrative style which is perhaps more dispassionate than dramatic, Mr. Gill tells of life as it is, not as we might like to think of. There are no traditional heroes or villains in his short stories; only real people reacting to the basic situations which are to be found in all corners of this global village. No doubt this is why Mr. Gill's characters come across with such authenticity.

This collection of short stories covers a wide range of topics in an equally wide range of settings. It tells us that people the world over have the same hopes and fears, the same problems and ambitions. In this book we can learn something of the universality of life; and we are enriched by that knowledge.

Russ Dewar
Managing Editor
The Standard-Freeholder

LONDON TO OTTAWA

The VC 10 was flying majestically over the Atlantic at an altitude of four thousand feet and a speed of more than five hundred miles per hour. A handful of passengers were busy gossiping, while others were enjoying the view below, where milk-like white fragments of cloud were floating. Some sober faces seemed buried in reveries as was his own whose uneasy imagination was hovering around the University of Ottawa.

After a long and boring journey of about seven hours, the landing of the aircraft at Montreal was announced, and with that his anxiety grew worse. It was five o'clock, and the problems which normally harass a foreigner began to torment him. He wanted to reach Ottawa before noon in order to have time to contact the university authorities for a suitable place to stay. He had approached the BOAC office in London for a reservation on a morning flight, but had failed to get help because Air Canada and the

LONDON TO OTTAWA

BOAC flights had been fully booked a fortnight before, owing to Expo'67. Under the circumstances he had to accept whatever was available; registration at the university was to take place on September 14th and he was already late, as he had been held up waiting to obtain his visa. It was imperative that he be at the university at least three days before registration to make the necessary arrangements.

The next flight from Montreal was at 8:30 p. m. , which meant he would arrive at Ottawa at about nine o'clock. He shuddered to think of trailing unknown streets of a strange capital at night. He was tired; every limb was complaining against a state of utter exhaustion. Two nights' sleep sacrificed at the altar of preparations and some other worries had already disturbed his psychic being. The unbearable and inhospitable warmth of the weather added to his distress. The thought of wandering about in search of a reasonably cheap lodging, carrying so much luggage, was haunting him like a ghost. After thinking carefully, he decided to break the journey in Montreal and proceed to Ottawa the next morning. Timidly, and with a forced friendly gesture, he asked one of the BOAC men to arrange an overnight stay for him, but the answer was negative. He attempted to phone some hotels; even this resulted in nothing. All the hotels were booked up by Expo visitors. Something like despair invaded his soul. He determined to face up to the reality of the situation and went to the Air Canada office again.

There was still time for the plane. It was terribly stuffy and suffocating. He opened the door and slipped outside to breath fresh air. It was delightfully refreshing. The invigorating breeze acted as a tonic on his tired nerves. After a few minutes the aeroplane landed and the passengers were asked to board. He followed the crowd without thinking much. At the entrance to the jet he was greeted by the stewardess, who seemed to sense his misery and smiled to alleviate it. He hurriedly returned her smile, and proceeded further to look for a comfortable seat. He found one vacant in the middle of the craft. A charming woman was seated on the adjacent seat. She looked at him as if he were not a stranger. The man felt somewhat hesitant at first, but soon mustered courage and put his three pieces of luggage under the seat. There was insufficient room. Perceiving his difficulty, she placed one of his bags under her seat in front of her own. Her way of assisting the man was enough to encourage him to open conversation. Little by little he told her all his anxieties and problems. It gave him a good deal of relief to talk to someone. She was enormously sympathetic, like a friend. She also had a most graceful figure. The way she spoke made the man her willing captive. That was the first time during the dreary and tiresomely long journey that he forgot his fears. He was perspiring, but the heat was quite tolerable now, and his fatigue miraculously vanished. He felt infinitely energetic and animated. She told the man she was a nurse and he did not question it, for she had nursed his whole being. He would have liked the journey to continue forever. After a few minutes they became informal and intimate friends. Just as the giant of the man's obsession was lulled to sleep and he was in the realms of delight, the captain informed them that they were about to land. He felt as if he had been awakened from an enchanting dream. He became more perplexed and disturbed over the sad separation from his companion than he was over finding accommodation.

The aircraft landed and the passengers came out one by one. As he entered the magnificient terminal building, he read something written in green lying on a table : "Overseas Students Reception!" His heart leapt with joy. He met the volunteers of the "International League." Their cordiality and amiability were matchless. He took leave of his former companion and came into the fold of the receptionists. He was taken to their office in a Fiat, which ran on a broad, smooth, silent road, while his mind was circling around London, where a few hours ago he was struggling to solve some of his problems. He remembered Mary and her brother Dick and their parents who bade him a warm English farewell at London Airport. The scene abruptly changed and he found himself in New Delhi, Addis Ababa, Athens, Frankfurt and Rome in turns. It was an awesome wonder to have been in so many different countries within such a short span of time. Life stretched before him like the non-ending street on which their car was travelling, and the world emerged like a big village of people of diverse tastes, yet basically very alike.

AUNT DISAPPEARS

Hector saw Emma alighting from the car with her husband. He went to tell her that their aunt was not in, and that he had been there for over an hour. Baffled and worried, they looked around in the gloom of the evening. Mr. and Mrs. Gardner were passing that way. They asked them if they knew where their aunt could be. Mrs. Gardner told them she saw her two days ago. They tried to alleviate their anxiety by saying that she must be at someone's home.

Emma said, rather nervously, "There seems to be something wrong. You must hurry and inform the police."

"Let's wait a little more. It's not a problem to find her in a small village like this," Hector replied.

In a flash, Hector remembered that their aunt used to keep the door key under a large stone, which was still there. He went to it. The key was exactly at the spot where she used to keep it when he was a child. Inside the house, they saw a half finished cup of tea on the table and dishes left undone, which indicated that the aunt had left home in a desperate hurry. It was unusual to see no sign of decoration. Hector asked Emma to look for something to prepare meals, and he went out in search of his aunt.

Monkview was a small village of two hundred families. With the exception of a paved road, electricity and a large bungalow for the pastor, the technological development had not brought any conspicuous change to this part of the farmers' world. As the village was located on a hill it presented a beautiful sight, particularly in the summer. Emma and Hector were born and raised here. Their father was killed in the First World War, and their mother fell victim to a fatal influenza which broke out after the war.

On her death-bed, Mrs. Cox asked her sister Ruth to look after the children. Ruth never married, and brought up the children as her own. Later, Emma married a bank's accountant. Hector became a teacher in an elementary school in the same city where Emma lived with her husband, about a hundred miles from their village. They always celebrated the New Year with their aunt — a tradition which they followed almost religiously. Their aunt used to make special preparations to receive them, decorating the home for the occasion. It was the first time she was absent from home in such a way.

It was pitch dark. The barking of the dogs was breaking the night's silence intermittently.

He knew every inch of the land. Perceiving light from the church, he stepped towards it. At the gate Mrs. Price exclaimed, "Hey Hector, when did you come?"

"About two hours ago. I'm looking for my aunt."

Mrs. Price came closer to whisper, "She was seen recently with Ted. You know him, my child. He is the one who killed his wife and spent twenty years in prison."

"When did you see her last with him?"

"People saw her going to his house two or three times last week. I am sorry to say that Aunt Ruth keeps a murderer's company."

Thanking Mrs. Price, he headed towards Ted's home. All sorts of unpleasant thoughts were crowding his mind. Ted was a mysterious character. The villagers had conflicting opinions about him. As a matter of fact, no one knew why and how he had killed his wife. When he returned, after twenty years, he was a changed person. He began to love seclusion.

The door was opened by a middle-aged, energetic man. He said, "I am Hector. Is aunt Ruth in?"

"Come in."

Hector saw her sitting beside a woman. Close by Ted was lying in the bed with eyes almost closed. Aunt kissed Hector and then introduced the man who opened the door as Ted's brother, and the woman as his wife. In a few

20

minutes, Hector took leave of them. Outside the house he asked his aunt, "You keep a murderer's company!"

"I see him as a human being. Ted has cancer of the stomach. He was lonely and crying with pain for the last two days. He needed assistance. His brother came about an hour ago from the city."

"Anyhow, we have decided to take you with us to the city."

Pointing towards the east she said, "Nearly forty years ago I buried your grandfather there, and ten years after that your grandma. Within a few years your mother died. How can I leave them here alone? This village, and particularly our house, awaken nostalgic memories of my past."

Hector knew that his aunt loved the village as a mother would her children. In answer he simply smiled, looking at her wrinkled face.

A PATHAN SOLDIER

The infant raised his tiny soft hands, giving a
sweet smile, as Daud Khan took his machine-
gun to fire at close range. Perhaps the infant
thought the man was offering him a toy. Close
by, its parents were lying besmeared with blood.
With queer feelings Daud Khan's hands trembled
and the room began to spin before his eyes. He
was about to turn away when he heard the captain
shouting, "You, coward!" Like lightening the
captain rushed forward and finished the job with
his Chinese revolver. Daud Khan wished to snatch
the captain's weapon to kill him instead. Instantly
he realized he was in the military where such
actions are intolerable.

When the evening approached, Daud Khan
returned to the Dacca camp with the other soldiers. At supper, all of them enjoyed telling one
another the stories of their kills. Daud Khan
was in no mood for this; he wanted to think. The
infant reminded him of his own son whom he left
in his village. At the same time, the action and
the words of the captain were torturing him. It

was disgraceful for his tribesmen to attack a woman, an unarmed man, or anyone else treacherously. He remembered his vital and tall grandfather who once gave a night's rest to a stranger, whom he recognized in the oil-lamp's dim glow as his sworn enemy. That night the man was simply his guest, and therefore his grandfather treated him warmly in the tradition of Pathan's hospitality. In the morning, he bade him farewell with due respect.

Daud Khan was the only one from his tribe to join the army. His conscience often pricked him for deserting his centuries-old traditions, some of which are bravery and love for freedom. Before Daud Khan was sent to Bangladesh he was told by his Punjabi officer that the Bengalees had joined non-believers to destroy the religion and integrity of Pakistan, and that he was being sent to Dacca on a mission which was to save the nation and its creed.

While musing, Daud Khan saw Captain Ayub coming towards him. He said, "You must be wondering why I shot the child?" Daud Khan nodded his head, indicating his ignorance. Twisting his moustache, the Captain explained, "When these orphans become adults they would come to know the murderers of their parents. This would make them the worst enemies of our nation and would involve the country in never-ending warfare. Besides, there is the problem of feed-

ing and clothing them. " By this time more soldiers had gathered to listen to Captain Ayub, but
before he could go further the city of Dacca was
plunged into darkness. Obviously, the guerrillas had done it to terrorize the government and
to show their increasing strength. It made the
soldiers alert and many of them nervous. Captain Ayub rushed to his barracks to give orders
to be ready to face any eventuality, though he
knew that guerrillas would not dare enter the
camp of the military, fully-armed with sophisticated weapons. In a mood of indifference to
his environment, Daud Khan left his colleagues.

Having wandered for a while, he sat on the
ground under the starry sky. He imagined himself in Miran Sha, the village where he was born
and raised. Miran Sha was situated on a moun-
tain, along the border between Pakistan and
Afghanistan. Despite the conveniences and the
might which the British Government had, the
people of Miran Sha and of the surrounding villages, forming parts of Waziristan, could not
be subjugated. All the Pathans defied British
control. At the same time, they were segment-
ed into many tribes; some of which were blood-
thirsty of one another. It was not uncommon for
a father on his death-bed to urge his children to
be cautious of particular tribes or to take re-
venge on a specific person for the death of a
family member. Sometimes, two or more Pathan
tribes would engage in regular warfare, taking

positions on rocky mountains with the guns which were locally manufactured and sold openly in markets. Within a few hours, hundreds of dead bodies would litter the landscape. The British authorities used to fly helicopters and aeroplanes very low to drop bombs, mainly to threaten and sometimes to scatter the belligerents.

Miran Sha had a fort, within which life was disciplined and orderly. The fort had the office and residence of the political agent, the highest representative authority of the government. Also, it had a few aircraft, a jail, the police headquarter, office of the treasurer and houses of the prominent government officials who needed safety and protection. Occasionally, lawbreakers and suspects were jailed. Once a woman was arrested, along with some men. This action brought many armed Pathans to the fort. They asked the political agent to free the woman by the next morning or be ready to face the consequences. They further added that if the police wished, they could put more men behind the bars. The Pathans would not tolerate the imprisonment of a woman, because she was a symbol of honour for them. When the political agent realized the seriousness of the situation, he ordered her immediate release.

As soon as the woman joined her tribesmen awaiting her outside the fort, bullets coming from different directions ended her life. To keep their tribe's honour they had preferred to have the woman released, but once she was out many doubts assailed them. They began to think that she had stayed with strangers. She could have been easily dishonoured. They would have her dead rather than hear the gossip and back-biting of other tribesmen concerning her.

All of a sudden, Daud Khan began to long for mountains, orchards of apples, almonds and grapes, and for the freedom to roam over rocks and through valleys. He was distracted when he heard screams and entreaties. He saw two young women, not very far from him, being forcefully led to the camp by two soldiers. He took his revolver and felled the men.

He was delighted to free the women who ran frantically towards the main street, away from the military camp. As he watched them, a bullet hit his left shoulder. A fountain gushed from the wound. Slowly he moved his head to one side, while lying on the ground. He saw Captain Ayub standing, holding a gun a few yards from him. Using all his remaining strength, Daud Khan weakly lifted his revolver and aimed it at the captain. With that, darkness clouded his vision. He opened his eyes for a second to glance at the dying captain. A gleam of pride swept over his face and then he closed his eyes for ever.

TWO VOTARIES

Sitting alone on a rock, he often glanced at the lake whose water was being bathed in moon-beams. When the stars began to disappear, he once again retraced his footsteps towards his village. Any person of moderate understanding could sense that he was no stranger to that place. It was actually his wont to visit the shore frequently in search of his lost peace.

One night, while roaming in his customary manner, he saw a black horse near the lake. His heart leapt to his throat. Cautiously and fearfully he approached the rider who looked like a lunatic. His clothes were torn but clean, his hair disheveled, his face expressed humility. He moved towards the rider and asked him if he needed assistance. Laconically the stranger answered, "a few hours rest."

He brought the rider to his house, where he offered him a glass of home-made tej. When their eyes glowed with warmth, he asked the rider his name. Chuckling the stranger said,

TWO VOTARIES

"Ocbe."

"Where do you live Ocbe?" was his second question.

"Adi Quala — fifty kilometres from here," again he gave a short answer.

"What brought you here?"

"To find someone."

"Whom?"

"Oh! it's a long story," he said firmly, clutching the sides of his chair.

"But the story might have a title?"

"I myself am the title of this story."

"Strange!" The host muttered the word, looking towards the melting darkness of the night. Before he could add anything further, Ocbe spoke : "My story is long and the night is short. I expect you'll go to sleep before I finish it. At the same time, it is not pleasant to hear."

"I love to hear long stories." After a short pause, he continued, "My own story is a long one and still it is incomplete. However, I'll keep awake till your tale is over."

Ocbe looked into his empty glass. His host understood, and emptied the bottle into their glasses. Ocbe heaved a deep sigh, touched the tej to his lips ... looked again into the wondering eyes of his host and said, "This is a tale of my own destruction — of a girl whom I loved and lost. I met her for the first time at my brother's wedding. In a few minutes she won my

28

head and heart. After that we met a few times, but I could not open my heart to her. Whenever we met, I felt myself being weakened by her presence. In a few days she left our town. Before leaving, she gave me her address; her village is about two kilometres from here. She returned to her village, and with her went happiness. Her memory began to torment me day and night. One day, I decided to go to her with a proposal for marriage. It was Saturday. I still recall that night vividly. It was the month of June — a lovely Ethiopian season for fun and hilarity. The rain had just stopped, but lightning still flashed at short intervals, followed by occasional thunder. I planned to stay the night at an inn near her village and go to see her the next morning. I took my mare from the stable and set out for my destination. I was hardly a kilometre from the village when I realized the mare was tired and thirsty. I led her to a lake. Probably, it was the same one where you and I met a few hours ago. While the mare drank, I was taken aback to see two floating images in the lake. My hair stood on end. In the darkness images appeared like apparitions. In wonder, fear and curiosity, I looked at them attentively. These were the reflections of a girl and a boy making love to each other. A sudden flash of lightning revealed the girl's face clearly to me. It was slightly cool that night, but my body burnt with fire. It was as if many pounds of weight

29

had been heaped on me. I would have certainly fallen down had there not been a tree nearby against which I leaned for support. "

At this point the voice of Ocbe grew heavy and painful. Two drops rolled down his cheeks. He became silent for a while. The host's eyes also became tearful. Controlling his emotions, he ventured to ask, "Then what happened? Who was that girl? Tell me quickly." Glancing at his host's face Ocbe said, " She was the one to whom I was going to propose marriage. " After observing a short silence, he resumed:

"That was an unbearable sight. Mustering all my strength, I picked up a huge rock and struck my enemy while shouting wildly. The girl had seen me rushing towards her companion. She came in between us and the rock struck her. With a scream she fell to the ground. "

"Who was that other man and you have not told the girl's name as yet, " said the host.

"No, " he replied. "I cannot disclose who she is, for I don't want to defame and disgrace her. However, after the attack I became giddy. I was terribly frightened of being caught and hanged. Mixed feelings of jealousy and fear prompted me to kill the man. Before I could do so, he gave me a staggering blow which felled me. Soon I got up, rushed to the mare, and escaped. Neither of us could see the other's face. "

"The next day, early in the morning, police

came to our town searching for me. Without any reluctance I admitted my crime. I was sentenced to jail for life. Before her death, the girl begged the police to treat me with clemency. In prison I led an almost religious life which impressed my superiors. On their recommendation, I was released only yesterday. To meet the same man I have come here, for I was told he lives in this village. "

"That will not help you. "

"I want to beg forgiveness for my deed. Also, I want to leave my property to his children. After having done so, I'll pass the rest of my life in a monastry. This is the end of my story. Let us sleep now. "

"No my friend, this is not the conclusion. The story has just begun. "

"How?" Ocbe asked in great amazement.

"Listen, the girl whom you loved and killed was Neghisti. "

"Yes, but how do you know all this?"

"I am the person who was with her that night," he said with an emotion-filled voice.

"No, no. You can't be that man. You're telling a lie to get my property. "

"You must know that after Neghisti's death I did not marry. So, the question of having children does not arise. I am not greedy for your property," he cried.

"Can you please give any proof to support

TWO VOTARIES

your statement?" Ocbe spoke these words almost in one breath.

"Come along," he said. He took Ocbe into a room where Neghisti's picture was on an old table. She was smiling. Seeing the picture, Ocbe ran to it and embraced it, holding it close to his breast. Both the votaries were shedding tears.

WHAT A MISTAKE !

Meerut is one of the oldest cities and also was the first city of India to have mobilized rebellion against the British rule in 1857. The city is adorned with magnificient buildings, modern hotels and restaurants, to the glory of the affluent segment of society. Many of the restaurants, particularly moderately expensive ones, are frequented by university students, journalists, poets, story writers and intellectuals of other genres who love to carry on heated discussions over a cup of tea or an alcoholic drink. Side by side to it, there is a life of the swarming, uneducated slum dwellers. On the whole, the city gives the impression that women in any walk of life do not lag behind the men, and that the citizens are fully acquainted with international affairs, through the popular news media, which plays a large part in shaping their opinions.

Outside Meerut, the life of villagers offers an interesting contrast. The women-folk still

WHAT A MISTAKE !

use a corner of their sarees, their long loose dress, to hide their faces from strangers, their fathers-in-law and elder brothers of their husbands. The women are physically strong, vital, and feel proud of their work in the kitchen, rearing children and helping their husbands in fields. The wives normally keep themselves ten to twenty feet behind their husbands, while walking in the public places. Sometimes, this distance grows from thirty to fifty feet. At social functions, women join the company of women and men of the males. For centuries, the life in those villages has been rolling on, unchanged, in spite of the efforts of some to change it. In one of such villages Sita was born.

Like the other girls of the village, Sita was never sent to school. Whatever religious knowledge she had was imparted to her by the amateurish religious plays which were occasionally staged on festivals, from the talks of the Brahmins, and from her parents' conversation with other adults of the village. When she was fourteen-years-old her parents anxiety to find her a husband grew intense. At the age of sixteen the matter of her marriage became very serious for the whole family. Sita was by no means an unwanted child, nor did her parents lack the resources to feed and clothe her, but they feared the social stigma of having an unwed daughter. It was the custom in those surrounding villages to have daughters married, even

WHAT A MISTAKE !

before they reached the age of sixteen. If any parents failed to do so, the villagers found all sorts of faults with the girl and often with the family. To escape such a scathing criticism, Sita's parents directed most of their energy towards finding a suitable bachelor. Sita's maternal uncle, at a cattle fair, once told her father about a farmer who had a son of marriageable age. On his advice, Sita's parents secretly inquired about the background of the farmer's family, particularly his son's. When they were satisfied that the boy was a teetotaller, non-smoker, and was from the same caste with unblemished past, Sita's parents proposed to the farmer the marriage of their daughter to his son. This they did through a grocer of that village, whom Sita's uncle knew casually.

Her father's long, recent and late-night talks with his male relations over puffs from a hookah, made Sita suspicious of something going on concerning her. One of the reasons which made her think so was her own age. She often desired to catch some sentences about her prospective husband. One of her informants used to be her brother's wife, who had been with her parents for the last three weeks. On such occasions Sita ardently longed for her company.

After some haggling, the proposal of marriage was accepted. A Brahmin's assistance was sought to prepare a zodiacal chart, based on the names, dates and the times of births of

WHAT A MISTAKE !

the would-be bride and bridegroom. With the
help of the astrological map, the Brahmin fixed
a date and time for the betrothal and wedding.
By this time, Sita's brother's wife had returned from her parents' home. Sita began to
receive, through her, all the pertinent information about her marriage.

It was the month of March, a season when
most of the marriages in north India are held.
Sita was sitting in a perfumed bed, decorated
with fresh flowers, wearing a long, thick veil,
which hid her face completely. She could hear
women singing to drum beats, intermittently
mixed with bouts of laughter. Long and wea-
risome centuries-old rites, performed before
and after the wedding, almost exhausted her.
It was midnight on the clock hanging in front of
her. Its regular, monotonous clicks were
breaking the room's stillness. Her eyes were
heavy, yet she wanted to keep awake in expec-
tation of her husband, who might enter any
time. While going around the sacred fire,
amidst chanting of the pandit's hymns, she
could catch a glimpse of him.

Like the other girls of her village Sita often
dreamt of a husband who would make her shy
by praising her beauty, and she would feign
anger. With different devices, the man would
bring her round. She also imagined herself
surrounded with children and an affectionate
husband. Now that long-awaited man was com-

WHAT A MISTAKE !

ing. Any moment she would hear the opening of the door, a hand lifting the veil from her face, and a soft voice speaking to her like one deeply in love. She began to think about how she should behave at that moment. She had heard some stories of the nuptial nights from her friends, and there were not many of them to tell. Also, there was hardly anything in common in those tales. She thought of the days when she would be back in her village to visit her parents, and how the virgins would ask her eagerly about her experiences. Like them, she had never met any man so far, and had not been kissed by anyone, except by her mother and father, and that only when she was a child. While thinking of these things, Sita heard the sound of someone entering. Her heart leapt to her throat. She could feel her hands and feet becoming cold. All her efforts to control herself failed.

He stopped for a moment beside the bed, and then softly removed the veil. After staring for a second, he said, "What a mistake!" In a few minutes she heard the doors closing. Soon he returned, but by this time Sita was emotionally torn apart. Therefore, she could not give what was expected of her. The next day when she got up, she had become fully convinced that marriage had turned contrary to her wishes. She had no complaint against the amount of work she had to do in the kitchen and in the fields. Actually, her parents had shaped her to this sort of

life. It was the indifference and apathy of her
husband which was unbearable. One night she
amassed her entire courage to ask,

"Why did you say the first night 'What a
mistake!'"

"I always thought that my wife would be pretty like a queen."

"You ought to blame your parents for that."

Ignoring the question, he continued, "Two or
three times when I took wheat to the city mar-
ket, I sneaked into movies. The movies had
pretty girls in them. I began to wish for a wife
like one of them."

"My parents never took me to any movie."

He became thoughtful for a while and then
spoke, "I am happy that you are hard-working
and patient like a cow. You can be pretty, if
you try to be so."

Sita had never used face powder. No girl
did so in her village. As a matter of fact, cosmetics were unknown there. The problem was
not only how and from where to procure the cosmetics, it was how to use them. She had not
even seen a woman using them. If she dared to
use cosmetics, she would become the talk of the
village the next day. As far as dresses were
concerned, they were traditional, like the ones
used by the rest of the women of the village.
It was not so easy to go against the accepted
norms of the farmers. She therefore decided
to leave herself to circumstances, accommodat-

WHAT A MISTAKE !

ing herself to whatever fate had to offer.

Within a year, Sita gave birth to a lovely baby girl. She was waiting for this day in the hope that the child would help fill the gulf created by her husband's whim. The child could not be of any help, rather it deepened their dissensions. Sita's husband wanted her to give birth to a boy. One day, he clearly told her that he would send her back home for good if she delivered a girl again.

Sita's every attempt to please her husband failed completely. She did not want to break up the marriage under any condition, because it would cast a slur on her. She knew that the gossips and backbitings of the people would render her life miserable. No one would try to understand her. She began to condemn herself, thinking that she was not needed anywhere, and therefore she should end her life. The thought of her child prevented her from taking this final step. She thought her sufferings were perhaps the outcome of her previous life's sins. If God appears before me, I will ask Him my faults. She knew girls who were far less beautiful and no healthier than she was, and yet, those girls were adored by their husbands, like the goddess Lakshmi. At the pride and indifference of her husband, she wept many times. On numerous occasions, she cursed her fate and asked Lord Siva forgiveness of the sins of her past life. She also consoled herself by blaming God for

WHAT A MISTAKE !

her plight. But none of these devices improved their disintegrating marital relations.

In the whole village, the only person who seemed to like Sita was Aunt Durga, a married woman of forty years, and very talkative. She was aunt to everyone, for no apparent reason. She used to tell Sita about men and women of the village. Many of her stories appeared to be fictitious or exaggerated. More than once, she told Sita that she did not look happy, and asked if there was anything she could do for her. Sita loved to hear stories from her, but at the same time decided to keep quiet about her personal affairs. She feared that Aunt Durga might reveal their talks to others. Whenever Aunt Durga showed concern for her, Sita pretended to be happy.

One morning when Sita went to the village well to draw water as usual, she decided to take the risk. Cautiously and slowly, she told Aunt Durga that her husband wanted a boy at her next delivery, otherwise he would send her back home. Looking into Sita's eyes, Aunt Durga advised her to bring a relic from the holy man, who lived about two miles from there. Sita had heard about such men who blessed many. When she was very young, her brother's toddler became sick. A holy man cured him in seconds, simply by blowing into his forehead. She recalled the incident of a barren woman who had a child because a holy man prayed for her. At the

WHAT A MISTAKE !

village fair, she once saw a man who used to sleep on sharp, pointed nails. At the same fair, she saw a thin and lean man walking bare-foot on fire. Many barren women of her village used to visit a holy man who gave them prayers written on papers folded and wrapped in a metal container. The women wore them around their necks or arms, and as a result of it had children. Many men, women and children got rid of evil spirits by touching the hands of those holy persons. She had heard also of the swindlers. In any case, she did not see any harm in trying Aunt Durga's advice.

One afternoon her husband had to stay longer in his fields for irrigation. Sita snatched time from her work and went to see the holy man. A strongly-built man of about fifty years was sitting in meditation in front of a cottage, surrounded by bushes. There was no village or house nearby. He wore a saffron-coloured gown, and on his forehead had marks of ashes. His long hair, hanging from his shoulders and his flowing beard were both dyed in saffron, indicating he had been leading that sort of life for years. Sita gently squatted to one side. In a few minutes he opened his eyes to ask,

"What do you want?"

"My husband has threatened to divorce me if I do not give him a son, holy man." Sita said the words mechanically and folded her hands together respectfully.

41

WHAT A MISTAKE !

The man took a pitcher carved from jungle wood or a dry vegetable. The pitcher was also saffron in colour. He poured a few drops from it into an earthen cup and handed it to her to drink. As Sita touched the cup to her lips, she detected a weird taste in the liquid. In no time, she swallowed it like the medicine administered to her when she was a child. The man closed his eyes, counting beads and counselling Sita to remain sitting for fifteen minutes, to let the liquid have its full effect on her. In a few minutes she felt dizzy and then became oblivious of everything.

On awakening, she tried to glance round the place. The man was in meditation with closed eyes as usual. She felt that certain parts of her body were snapped and twitched. As a result her lips and cheeks were burning. A front button was also missing. Without uttering a single word, she stood up and retraced her steps towards her village. It was almost dark. She could hear the dogs barking from afar. Literally she ran to reach her home before anyone realized she was absent. As soon as she entered her house she heaved a sigh of relief. Her husband was not in yet, and as far as her in-laws were concerned they had gone to see their relatives some days ago. Immediately, she went to the kitchen to prepare supper.

After about half an hour her husband came. Pretending anger, Sita asked, "Where have you

WHAT A MISTAKE !

been? The supper is getting cold. "

"You have to tell me first where were you?"

"I went to have a medicine. " Sita replied.

"What trouble do you have?" He spoke harshly.

"Not to have a baby boy. "

"What medicine have you brought?"

"He made me to drink in front of him. "

"Who?"

"The holy man. "

He looked at his wife meaningfully, and then rushed into the kitchen. He came out with a stick. Grasping the situation, she left the room from the other side. Sita heard the doors being slammed behind her.

Sita remained outside for an hour or so. When she realized that he was not going to open the door, she gave a slight knock at it. A voice asked,

"Who is there?"

"It is I. "

"If you want your life, go anywhere you wish. " He thundered.

She sat down and began to think of the possible steps she could take. The night's horrifying darkness and stillness had wrapped every object in its fold. The worst pang she had was for her child, who was still with her husband. She lost that pang in her yearning to have a few hours rest. Sitting alone in front of her own house, she felt completely worn out and incapa-

ble of anything but sleep. There was no trans-
portation available in the night to go to her parents, who lived about ten miles away. Once
again she remembered Aunt Durga. Slowly she
raised herself from the ground and headed towards Aunt Durga's home. The door was opened
by a man. Sita said,

"I want to see Aunt Durga."

"Come in, please."

Finding no one else in the house Sita said,
"Where is she?"

"She has gone to see the fair. It's nearly
time for her to come back."

For some time they carried on pointless
talks, in which both seemed to be disinterested
for their own reasons. When they were silent
for a while, the man said, "You appear to be
tired. Better lie down in Durga's bed. She will
be surprised to see you there."

Every part of Sita's body was aching, and
therefore she felt the need for rest badly. She
took the opportunity and went to Aunt Durga's
bed, where in no time she fell asleep. She opened her eyes when she felt something heavy on
her. In the gloom, her hands felt a beard-grown
face. She tried to get up, but strong arms threw
her back. When she attempted to cry, the palm
of his hands closed over her mouth. Realizing
that once again she had become a victim, she
surrendered herself to the time.

With the first cock's crow, she left the bed,

WHAT A MISTAKE !

though she was still sleepy. The events of the last day and the night were fresh in her memory. She looked around. Aunt Durga was nowhere to be seen. Softly, she lifted the latch and went out. While opening the door, she heard Aunt Durga's husband snoring.

It was dawn by the time she reached the border of the village. She saw a horse-driven carriage coming towards her. At her signal the coachman pulled on the reins to stop the horse. Sita asked the man if he was going to Mohidpur. As he was going farther than that, he asked Sita to get in.

There were five passengers in the carriage which was meant for only four. Sita occupied the rear seat between two women. The coachman whipped the feeble-looking mare with a heap of abuses, and the carriage began to move along the dusty track. All five passengers began to jostle and rock. It put Sita to sleep. She woke up when the man told her they had arrived at her village. From a tiny wallet which she herself had sewn from coarse cloth, she handed the coachman a few coins.

Sita saw her mother cleaning rice in the courtyard of her house. She rushed into her mother's arms as a child would, and wept bitterly. Seeing her daughter in a terrible state, the mother could not control her tears. When Sita was slightly relieved of her emotions, her mother offered her a glass of warm, sweet milk,

WHAT A MISTAKE !

which gave her energy. By that time everyone in the village had come to know of Sita's arrival without her child and husband. This unusual event provided the villagers with a subject of gossip for some days. Her father and brother had heard about her through someone in the fields. So far, her mother had not bothered her with any question. After having the milk, Sita herself began to tell her story. Within two days she told her parents everything she thought relevant. This made her parents grieve, and feel furious with her husband.

On the third day, her father, along with Sita's maternal uncle, met the grocer who had acted as an intermediary in arranging marriage. All three saw the elder of the village where Sita was married, to discuss the matter. The elder asked Sita's father-in-law to join their talks. Unitedly, they put pressure on Sita's husband to improve their marital relationship in future. Very little was said of the past. For hours they admonished both of them, quoting here and there the ideal men and women from the Indian scriptures and mythology. With their advice and persuasion, Sita went to live with her husband once again.

Sita noticed considerable change in her husband. He was no longer indifferent to her. At the same time, he appeared to be lonesome. Sita made special efforts to please him, and severed her relations with Aunt Durga.

WHAT A MISTAKE !

After three months, something peculiar happened in the village. One night when the whole family was in bed, Sita heard ferocious barks, which were followed by knocks at the door. Two huge dogs leapt on Sita's husband when he opened the door. He hastened inside to get his solid, long stick to kill the animals. A middle-aged man who was in police uniform got hold of him. With a strong jerk, Sita's husband threw the man on the floor. His two companions who held the dogs' chain came forward and helped the floored policeman control Sita's husband. All three succeeded in fastening handcuffs around the wrists of Sita's husband. Meanwhile, the elder of the village arrived with some men. The elder was told by the policemen that a hermit was murdered a few weeks ago. Following the blood stains on the ground, the dogs led the investigators to a grave in which the hermit's dead body was discovered. The corpse's face was wrapped in a blood-stained shirt, which belonged to the murderer. The same dogs, after smelling the shirt, led the investigators to this house.

According to the police report, Sita's husband had killed a holy man, but the police were unable to discover the homicidal intentions. Sita's husband maintained his silence about the murder. Perhaps he did not want his family to be disgraced through his wife's character. The only person who knew the secret besides him

WHAT A MISTAKE !

was Sita. She was right in thinking the truth would blacken her parents' name, bring shame to her daughter and also affect her daughter's marriage. She was determined not to divulge the truth under any circumstances.

Sita's father-in-law sold a part of his dearly-loved fields to save his son's life. Sita's father also parted with a piece of his property to assist his son-in-law. After some time, the elders of both villages came forward with their open support, as the life of Sita's husband became a matter of respect for the people of both villages. None of them were experienced in the complexities of court. On the one hand was the power of the law and its implementors, very proficient in their art; whereas on the other side were illiterate farmers, who knew only to obey their impulses. The struggle between the forces went on for a year. Towards the end, the farmers were defeated, and Sita's husband was sentenced to ten years' imprisonment. Sita went back to her parents once again. This time with her child.

THE YOUNGER BROTHER

Adi Ugri is a small town about seventy-five kilometres to the north of Asmara. In 1940, the town had an outbreak of influenza which proved fatal for many of its inhabitants. Girmaie was nine-years-old and his sister Lete thirteen, when their mother fell victim to this epidemic. Their father had lost his life four years ago, while fighting as a soldier, miles away in the army of Italians, who ruled Eritrea in those days. After his death, their mother shouldered the responsibility of educating her children. Now these two little lives were without shelter and hope. Lete had noticed, since the time of their mother's burial, two days ago, continual tears in her younger brother's eyes. Unable to bear this painful sight, she went to him, gently wiped his wet cheeks, held him close to her, and vowed to look after him as their mother had.

School no longer interested her. The next day, she locked her books in a box and started

doing odd jobs in a restaurant, where passing
soldiers and busloads of people often stopped
for beer, a cup of coffee, or a snack. Girmaie
continued his education with the help of his sister. He was happy and keen to reach his goal.
When he wrote his school-leaving examination,
his grave and gloomy face once again touched
the tender cords of his sister's heart. During
his childhood, their mother used to say she
would like to see Girmaie become a teacher. A
certificate of tenth grade would not be of much
help to achieve this aim. Girmaie did not see
how he could carry on his studies at the university, about five hundred kilometres from their
town. His sister did not make enough money to
cover his university expenses. She had thought
that after the tenth grade Girmaie would work;
this would give her security, and a sense of
relaxation and freedom. When her brother, at
supper time, discussed his intentions, Lete
became anxious, not for the drudgery of another
four years, but because she feared she would be
unable to meet his university expenses.

By the time Lete was a grown girl; many
tried to take advantage of her youth and loneliness. But she had only one purpose in life — to
support her younger brother in his education.
After many nights of thought, she decided to
marry the butcher of her town, if he would agree
to assist her brother. The butcher, in his four-
ties, had proposed to her many times before,

but she always turned down his offer. He often went to the restaurant where she worked, for a glass of beer and to watch her. The grace and indifference with which she served the customers made him her ardent admirer. This time Lete encouraged him to propose marriage, and when he did so, she accepted it with a condition to which he readily agreed.

The butcher kept his promise for about two years, after which he found it almost impossible to send money to Girmaie. His wife threatened divorce, which instead of softening him, made their relations more tense. He asked her to check his accounts. She discovered that her husband's business had considerably declined. Some Italians had set up business in competition. Their sophisticated and improved ways dealt a shattering blow to the industries run by the local people. Many had folded their shops to find remunerative jobs somewhere else. When Girmaie came home after his second year's examination, Lete made him aware of their distressing situation.

Girmaie disclosed to one of his friends his recent decision to find a job rather than go back to university. His friend hinted that instead of searching for a job, he should search for a rich man's daughter. Girmaie saw a ray of hope in the idea. Soon both the friends began to survey rich families. After some deliberation, they found out about a coffee-garden's owner who had a fat,

queer-looking daughter of marriageable age.
He was living in a town not far from the university. They had a friend in the same town.
Many times, on weekends, they went to see him.
It was during these visits they happened to see
this girl; her father lived next door to their
friend. With the assistance of his friend,
Girmaie contacted the owner of the coffee gar-
dens. He was pleased to accept the conditional
proposal, though he was known for his miserli-
ness. Within a month, the marriage was ar-
ranged and Girmaie once again entered the university. He left his sister's house to live at
his father-in-law's place. His sister was sad,
but also happy that her younger brother had
found the means to continue his studies.

Gradually, the day approached when he was
to obtain his master's degree in biology. His
hard work and amiable nature won him friends
among the professors. On their recommenda-
tions, he got a teacher's position within the university itself. During the holidays, his wife
urged that they should take a residence near the
university, away from her parents. Without
hesitation Girmaie consented to this. In the
new house she turned out to be very smart,
began to take an active interest in her household
affairs, and also financial matters. Girmaie
also began writing articles for newspapers and
periodicals. This spread his fame and brought
him fortune.

THE YOUNGER BROTHER

Girmaie's extra income did not make a change in his domestic life; all the money was taken away from him by his wife. Once or twice, he mildly protested against this, but she closed his mouth by saying he had no right to keep the money. Her attitude made him extremely unhappy. However, it was a great consolation to receive his sister's letters regularly. During this period, the butcher's business was on the verge of utter ruin. In her last letter, she asked Girmaie for some money to enable her husband to improve his business, in order to face the competition of the Italians. So far, he had not sent even the smallest present, either for his sister or her children.

It was about ten months since Girmaie started working, and he was still as poor as before. The day he received his next cheque from the editor of a newspaper for one of his articles, he determined to send this to his sister. He wrote a letter, left it on the table with the cheque, and went in for a shower. When he returned, he was stunned to see the letter torn into pieces and the cheque missing from the table. His wife, with an angry look, appeared from the other side of the kitchen. Before he could open his mouth, she thundered, "It is my father who financed your studies. Your relatives never showed their faces at that time. They have no right to ask for help now." These cruel remarks of his wife upset him terribly. Controlling himself, he tried to reason with her in a calm tone. But she would not listen. Without stopping, she kept on admiring her father and blaming his sister. Unable to bear her aggressiveness, he put on his suit and left for the university.

This last incident gave him a chance to scrutinize his whole life once again. He could by no means say he was better off than before. His pockets were as empty as ever; he still depended on his wife for his needs. He could not call anything his own even in his own house. He did not see any point in working harder to supplement his income. He felt of himself as a bird with clipped wings. The whole series of sacrifices made by his sister began to appear in his mind. The agony caused by his lack of gratitude became intense. He started condemning himself for his timidity and selfishness. He passed many days and nights in self-torment, brooding over the problems, and examining himself in the light of recent occurrences. The university became a refuge — he went home only to have his main meals and to sleep.

When his sister did not receive an answer, she began to worry. One evening, when he returned from the university, he heard his wife's voice, "Neither you nor your husband came to his help when he was needy. He came to us and it was my father's generosity that enabled him to earn, and ..." Girmaie's heart began to beat

THE YOUNGER BROTHER

fast. He hastened into the room. His sister
was sitting, listening calmly to his wife. She
looked mournful, no longer young and active.
A few years of suffering had made her look
older than her years. He remembered his days
with her after the death of their mother. He
rushed to hold her close to him. Both wept to
see each other after the lapse of two years.
Girmaie turned to his wife and said firmly :

"I have paid enough interest on the invest-
ment of your father. From today on, you will
get nothing from me." Saying this, he took his
sister's hand and stepped out of the house.

DETERMINATION

Liza's personality was a peculiar blend of old and modern ideas. To her it was painful to think of working outside the home after marriage. This was not the whim of a crank, but a resolution based on her education and observations. To her, it seemed that a woman earning her living could be neither a successful mother nor a helpmate. She was convinced that nothing can substitute a mother's affection and nearness to her children, which builds confidence in them and fortifies them to face life's distresses. Children brought up by babysitters can hardly identify with parental love, whose sacred cords bind a family together. She feared that, devoid of a mother's care, young ones are prone to neurosis, and easily led astray.

Woman's liberation movement to her was promiscuity in disguise; these women, sometimes dressed like men, resembled soldiers marching towards their own destruction. She considered herself as emancipator in the sense

DETERMINATION

of freeing herself from the clutches of ignorance, whereas the liberation movement was
ushering in a new ignorance. It gave her a feel-
ing of relief when she told Rejean again, and
even more emphatically this time, that she
would not work once she was led to the altar.
Her relationship with him was deep, she admir-
ed him, but at the same time could not relin-
quish her cherished convictions.

Rejean was an artist, and as such had deft-
ness and propensity to transform his imagination into lifelike forms. His ever-alive passion
for art went back to the time of his childhood
when he used to play with clay. Had he come
from a well-to-do family, he would have made
sculpture his life's pursuit. The surge of his
desire to rise and be recognized, in the area of
his inclination, was arrested by a constant lack
of money. He decided to marry one who would
be willing to support him, to let him have enough
time to realize his ambition. He met Liza at
the income-tax office, where forced by circumstances, she worked as a typist. The inadequate
salary of her father of nine children, and the
loan she had had from a bank to finance her
studies, obliged her to accept this position.
From a distance, Rejean perceived the emer-
gence of a new sun when he met Liza, whose
recent refusals to work after marriage left no
alternative but to watch the funeral of his pro-
clivity for a woman who regarded herself crea-

DETERMINATION

tive in her own way. In Liza's view, a mother creates nature, an artist copies it, and therefore she is superior to an artist, for he, unlike her, works with inanimate objects. She believed herself to be a genuine and better artist, who had the ability to mould the characters of living beings.

Within a year after their wedding, their conjugal bliss was doubled at the birth of a son. Rejean did not show any sign of joy, when after a few months of bearing their first child Liza became pregnant again. Being an ordinary clerk, it was beyond his means to meet the expenses of the next delivery, and of an increasing family. The money he had borrowed at the first child's birth was still unpaid. He therefore proposed planned parenthood. To this Liza would not agree. Instead, she asked him to find ways to supplement his income, to which he readily consented. The following evening, he returned with news of his success. From that day on, it became his routine to come home late in the night, even on weekends. He hardly had time to talk to his wife and child. Overwork and incomplete rest began to affect his health. Also, their predicament in no way improved, for he did not bring home the commission he made from his part-time employment. Realizing the price she had to pay, Liza began to insist on his leaving that job. He tried to console her by saying that the company settled accounts once a year and that they had to wait to get the sum owing them.

On her birthday, Rejean asked her to be ready for the next afternoon, for he would take her out to dinner and then they would go to an art exhibition. That day he took Liza to the Volga Hotel, a reasonably pleasant place, where they had a meal of roast chicken, their favourite dish. They were all infinitely gay. Liza seemed to be the happiest. It was part of her nature not to bother her husband with all sorts of unnecessary questions, a fact that had endeared her to him. Her suggestions and protests used to be few, and usually mild. At the art gallery, she kept herself busy, mostly with her child, giving her husband sufficient time to talk with the men who came to greet him on his arrival. One of them told him of the sale of a few art pieces for two thousand dollars, and said he hoped to sell more before the crowd melted from the gallery. Liza thought it was her husband's part-time job to arrange this exhibition. Before she could ask anything about it she noticed her son clapping hands with sheer joy to see beautiful images of different shapes and sizes chiselled in attractive curves. So that he might not be lost in the throng, she went to him— he was standing near a charming model of a woman holding her son to one side, a grown-up man stood on the other side, and an infant sat on her lap. Forcing her way through

DETERMINATION

the crowd gathered around this statue, she approached it. Her eyes fell on the name of the sculptor, written at the bottom. She did not trust what she saw there. Hurriedly, she ran her eyes over the other models; there she read the same name. Her lips parted with a smile, full of wonder and happiness. With the child, she rushed to Rejean, who understanding the reason of her unusual behaviour signalled her, indicating that she come out of the hall.

"When did you make them? Why didn't you tell me the exhibition is of your own art?" She burst out nearly in the same breath.

"You did not know, Liza, it was my ambition to be a great sculptor. I wanted you to work so that I could devote my time to art, but you refused to do so. When you asked me to supplement my income, I decided to try my luck here." He answered placidly.

"Why didn't you tell me this before? I would certainly have assisted you."

"I wasn't sure of my success. You should know, many flowers wither before they bloom; a few are able to scatter their fragrance before they die. Blessed are those, who achieve recognition in their lifetime."

Liza wanted to say something, but the words stuck in her throat.

FATE OR COINCIDENCE

Rajesh came to Canada with his wife before the slump, when immigrants had no difficulty in finding jobs. Citizens looked at the newcomers with respect and curiosity. Within two weeks of his arrival at Riverdale, Rajesh was offered an assistant engineer's position in a local electronic factory. Rajesh and his wife, Neela, liked this small town for its natural surroundings and the accessibility to a lake and river. Rajesh was a native of a village near Bombay, where swimming and fishing were the favourite pastime of most of the youth. In Riverdale, he pursued his hobbies on summer weekends.

On one such day, Rajesh went to the lake with his friends. As they were approaching the bank, after having swum to their hearts' content, he looked behind him. In the rays of the setting sun, he noticed something black rising out of the waves. Thinking it was a rock, he left his companions to have the fun of standing on it for a while. His friends heard a dreadful cry. They rushed to the neighbouring village for help. Many people came, but they could not find his body. Some said he was attacked by a monster, while others maintained that quicksand had sucked him down.

Rajesh's tragedy made Neela think of the inauspicious zodiac signs under which she was born. The Brahmins told her parents to donate cows to holy men and give alms to the poor to avert the evil effect of certain stars. Neela's parents had dismissed the Brahmins' advice as superstitious. Neela herself, like most educated Indian girls, regarded astrological theories as mere assumptions. Her husband's death shook her modern convictions.

The ten thousand dollars which Neela received from the insurance company were enough to give her economic security for some time. Since she had no child to look after, it was easier for her to further her education in order to compete for a good job. A few months after Rajesh's death she applied for admission to an M. A. programme, and for a scholarship at a university in Alberta. She obtained both without difficulty. On the campus she met men of all sorts and of different nationalities. Some of them invited her for tea or dinner, while others asked her to dance at clubs or parties. Neela was brought up in an environment where widows had no future and even unmarried girls were derided if they went out with boys. She was thousands of miles away from that society and was free to shape a new life in the way she desired. Neela often thought that one of the Canadians would make a desirable husband. In some Canadian families, she had noticed the husbands helping their wives in the kitchen. In the social sphere they are known for giving more freedom to their wives than Indian husbands do. Neela was very cosmopolitan, yet she had no courage to accept any non-Indian as her boy friend. At times, she was discouraged by the ill feelings it might engender in her compatriots. Whenever one of them approached her for a date, an unknown fear invaded her.

The fear of the unknown did not stand in her way when Rahul, from India, asked her for a cup of tea at the university cafeteria. The first invitation paved the way for many more, and each led them towards a mutual understanding. Gradually, Neela began to open her heart. She told Rahul about the evil influence of stars on her life, about the holy Brahmins' advice and her first marriage. Rahul laughed these doubts away, telling her that the Brahmins' zodiacal chart was irrational and her husband's tragedy was a coincidence. He offered Neela his love and she happily accepted it.

Once again, Neela became a wife. Rahul was a professor of physics at the same university where Neela went for her studies. He felt a peculiar attraction to Neela's youthful, sober look. Two or three times Rahul and Neela went to Riverdale to pass a few days in the quiet atmosphere there. Rahul liked the place. He resigned his job at the university, which was very far from Riverdale, to become head of the department of physics at the Riverdale Community College. He called Naresh, his younger brother, from Bombay, who enrolled as a first year student. From her husband, Neela received love, and from Naresh, respect. Rahul brought in the money and she looked after the home. Naresh often helped her with grocery shopping and ordinary housework. Life appeared to be cheerful and smooth.

After Rajesh's death, Neela had developed a fear of water. She always discouraged Rahul from swimming. One stuffy and sticky afternoon in July, Rahul went with Naresh to a river without informing his wife. He simply told her to keep supper ready, that they would be back in an hour or so. They chose a solitary spot and began to enjoy their swim, forgetting the heat of the day. Naresh was ahead of Rahul. He was suddenly caught in a whirlpool. He cried out for help, raising his hand. Rahul rushed to him, but the currents were stronger than they. Some men in a canoe saw them struggling and disappearing in the turbulent water. They guided their canoe towards them. Meanwhile, more help arrived from the other direction. They were quite dead by the time their bodies were found. Nothing could bring them back to life.

Neela was busy in the kitchen, when she heard people talking in front of her home. She was so occupied with her work that she paid little attention. However, their persistent talk distracted her. From the window she saw some men looking towards her door. Curiosity brought her outside. One of the men asked her if she would identify two dead bodies. As she neared the station wagon, the man removed the cloth from their faces. Neela swooned and fell to the ground. When she opened her eyes, darkness had already descended.

Neela's father-in-law was a lawyer in India. He asked her to live with him. He promised to care for her as his own daughter. Her father wrote her with the same offer. Neela knew that in her home town she would be looked upon as one possessed by demons. Mothers would deter their children from coming near her; newlyweds would keep her at a distance. She would be avoided at festive occasions to avert the shadow of her evil star. This might not be obvious all the time, but she would sense it. Neela therefore decided to stay in Canada, alone, without making any further attempt to seek conjugal bliss. She was almost convinced that no man dare propose to her, nor would she like to endanger anyone's life again.

ENIGMA

He had been upset since early morning. The child's cries and his wife's demands before leaving for the office, broke intermittently into his thoughts on the day's work he had planned. After his wife left, he rushed to his writing desk carrying a cup of tea; the sketch in his mind grew hazy and vague. He forced himself to write a few sentences, but the pen was unwilling to cooperate. On such occasions he normally stretched out on the bed or sofa with his eyes closed to muse over the subject. As he lay on the bed, the telephone rang. He jumped to grab the receiver. Hardly had he said "hello" when someone said,

"May I talk to Mr. Antonio Petrucci, please."

"Speaking." He was going to add, "What can I do for you?" when he realized that there was nothing in the world he could do for a girl. He had neither time nor money, nor was he a bachelor. He had been so deep in thoughts that he gave barely half of his attention. He interrupted the caller,

"May I ask who's speaking?"

"This is Ann Rock from the Bytown Library. We have a few openings for catalogue clerks. We would be pleased to consider your application, if you are still unemployed," was the answer.

He made a note of the information Ann gave him and went back to his desk after thanking her. By now all the ideas for the day's writing had vanished from his mind. Abandoning the attempt to create anything new, he picked up one of his old short stories to revise. He was happy to receive the news. In the three years since his immigration to Canada, this was the first time someone had called him about a job. He had sent applications to many offices — in some cases he saw the officials personally. The result was always the same. He was put off with one excuse or another. To be honest, he was never called for an interview, nor were his references ever contacted.

At two o'clock Antonio went to the Bytown Library. He asked a receptionist at the front desk if he had a form 70IM for Antonio Petrucci. The receptionist asked Antonio his name, looked him over from top to toe, then led him to a hall which was divided with plywood panels into many small cubicles. In spite of these partitions, the cubicles afforded no privacy to the occupants. Each cubicle contained a table and two chairs. While crossing the hall he glanced around. The clerks, pretending to be busy, looked at him as if he were an intruder in their land.

The receptionist left him in an empty cubicle. Antonio took a chair to wait for the woman who had called him on the phone. Within a few minutes she emerged, smiling. She stretched out her hand, introducing herself as Mrs. Rock. Antonio heaved a sigh of relief. It was his experience that most women have only one objective in their minds— to look for their prospective husbands. In this age of women's liberation and women's equality it might sound paradoxical, but for him it was a fact. Mrs. Rock's marital status made him feel that her assistance would be impartial.

Mrs. Rock was a pretty woman of about thirty. She had dignity and a special friendliness in her manner. Her face was fresh as a new blossom; her mature and well-developed body captivating. Sitting in the chair she said,

"I am replacing Mr. Robinson."

"I wish you had replaced him long ago."

"You mean ..."

"You are going to bring me luck, it seems."

Her eyes sparkled. Smilingly she said, "Keep your fingers crossed."

After this they had a delightful chat. She told Antonio she had recently been transferred from Montreal. At this point she asked, almost abruptly,

"May I know what brought you to Ottawa?"

"My wife works here."

"Oh ! — you are married? It is not men-
tioned in your application." There was surprise
in her look.

"I was not married when I filled out the
form."

She became serious. In a business-like
manner she began to explain the job for which
he was going to be considered. Their talk became shorter and to the point. The interview
was the next day and he was offered a position.

The Bytown Library is located on the ground
floor of a skyscraper. In the small office on the
left of the entrance there is always someone
available to assist visitors. A few steps further
up there is a catalogue desk, where Antonio
works most of the time. Still further up, there
is a door to a small office. This is the room
where Mrs. Ann Rock works as an assistant
librarian. For many days after Antonio's ap-
pointment he did not see her. Often he snatched
time from his work, hoping to converse with
her for a while, but there was always someone
with her. She appeared to be indifferent, unlike
the person he met on the first day. She became
an enigma for him. The more he thought of the
enigma the more incomprehensible it grew.

One morning when he was busy sorting
cards, he heard footsteps approaching. He

turned round to see Mrs. Rock near him. She asked Antonio if he enjoyed his work. He took the opportunity to tell her,

"I have written a short story about you. "

"About me ! She became serious. "We talked only for a few minutes when we first met. "

"That was enough to start the foundation. "

"You need material also for the building. " She replied.

"I leave that to my imagination. "

"Show it to me please, when it is finished. " She turned and left.

For a week Antonio did not see her — she was as busy as ever. Often she smiled from a distance, but never left her work to come to him. One day during the lunch hour he was sitting alone in the cafeteria. He saw her coming. She was as pretty as usual. In her customary way she asked permission to share his table. Sipping from her cup of coffee, she asked about the story. Antonio told her it was ready. He invited her to a restaurant after office hours the next day for a drink, where he proposed to read the story to her. Instead, she asked Antonio to come to her apartment for dinner. Prompted by a hunch, Antonio asked if her husband worked in Ottawa. She said, "I forgot to tell you that I'm divorced. " This short answer solved Antonio's enigma.

TOYS

On her face, smiles were rare and laughter non-existent. I had seen her often at departmental functions and in crowds; she always looked lost to me. Yet, her tall and well-developed physique and serious appearance were fascinating. During coffee breaks and lunch hours she liked to stay in her office, or else she would choose a lonely place in the cafeteria. The other day, I saw her at a distance while I was buying my lunch. She was sitting at the extreme corner table, sipping from a cup of coffee. A stray kitten happened to emerge from somewhere. She picked it up and began to pet it and stroke its back. The unique thrill which she experienced while doing so was apparent by the expression on her face. I felt impelled towards her.

After saying "hello" I asked if I could share the table with her. "Please", she uttered the word, still playing with the animal. After a few minutes' pause she spoke,

"Isn't it cute?"

"I have no liking for them." When it seemed that she would not reply I continued,

"I prefer dogs because they are faithful, unlike cats."

"It depends much on training, I suppose."

"Also on nature," I persisted.

Before she could comment, a couple occupied the adjacent seats. The couple's arrival coincided with the expiry of the lunch break. I gave a quick glance at my watch, then left the table saying "sorry" while chewing the last morsel of hamburger which I had literally thrown into my mouth.

After three or four days I saw her at a bus station. I stopped my Chevrolet to offer her a ride. She declined the offer politely, telling me that Fred was coming from Europe, and she was going to the airport to meet him.

I saw her many times with Fred in the following two weeks. He was tall, handsome, in his late thirties. I was certain that Fred could be no other than her boy-friend or a fiance, whose absence made her unhappy. There was no doubt that in his company she was relaxed and cheerful. However, the cheerfulness did not last long. She was alone again. Presumably, Fred had left her.

She was at Laroque's Store when I met her the next time. Two days of continual freezing rain and snow had paralyzed city traffic. It was

TOYS

not really cold, though the temperature had dropped to twenty below. Treacherous and messy streets had rendered driving hazardous. On such occasions, I spent most of my time watching TV or reading. I would not have gone out that day, but I needed a present for my niece whose birthday was to be on Sunday. Thinking the weather might grow worse by Saturday, I went out to shop at Laroque's, a place considered ideal for children's wear.

As I passed a show case, the "hey" of a familiar voice alerted me. I turned round. She was there examining toys. Both pockets of her coat were stuffed with toys, which she had bought perhaps from some other store. We talked about the weather and children's playthings. I discovered she had a wide knowledge of toys, at least much more than an average man has. When we were shopping, she asked me if I could give her a ride back home; I readily agreed to it. She purchased many toys and helped me buy a china doll for my niece.

When I returned home, I found she had dropped two tiny dolls on the car seat. I was not in the mood to go back and return them at nine o'clock at night, particularly in such miserable weather. I postponed it until the next day. At five in the evening, I drove to her home. The door was opened by an old lady, who later introduced herself as her aunt. The first thing she asked me was to come in. In the living room, where we sat opposite each other, she told me her niece had gone to the mental hospital.

"Mental hospital?" My whole being expressed a question. Noticing my amazement she said,

"Sandra's husband had a car accident on the second day of their marriage. The accident didn't cause as much physical injury as it caused damage to his brain nerves. When he opened his eyes after a three day coma, he was insane. His condition hasn't improved a bit. Normally on Saturdays she goes to see him. Sandra is very unfortunate. A few weeks ago her brother came to see them from Europe."

For some time I said nothing. Suddenly I broke the silence, remembering something, "Where are the children?"

"Which children?" She asked curiously.

"I mean those toys she bought yesterday!"

"I know what you mean. It's Sandra's favourite pursuit. I will show you her room."

I followed her to a room upstair. She opened the door gently. Toys were oddly arrayed on the book-shelf, table, fire-place, near the window, in the corner. These were of all sorts, colours and shapes. I turned my head to look at her. In an emotion-filled voice she said,

"Don't go without having a cup of coffee. You may sit in the living room. I won't be long." Slowly, we came down and she turned to the kitchen. As I entered the living room, I saw Sandra already there. "Hey, Mr. Murphy! When did you come?" She burst out in a mixed tone of joy and surprise.

"Just half an hour ago. Last night you forgot your dolls in my car. I have brought them back. By the way, how is your husband?"

Her look indicated that she knew her aunt had told me all about her. Instead of answering my question she came closer. Dropping her head on my shoulder, she began to sob as a child does.

ANOTHER TRAP

Her breasts, covered with sharp teeth bites, looked cold and white like marble. In front of him, the murmur of a canal was breaking the night's stillness. He slipped out of the Impala and headed towards the corner of the park. When he reached the narrow entrance, he halted for a moment to look round. In a flash he was on the road, from where he went to the main street. He stopped a taxi coming from the opposite direction and went to Billy Hill.

Billy Hill was not crowded like other parts of the city. One could see old, dilapidated houses which were still inhabited. For him, the only attraction the place afforded was its profound silence. He had been living there for the past six months, since he had first arrived at Calgary. No one knew his past occupation, nor the place from where he came. It did not take very long for the taxi to reach there. He entered his apartment, placidly lighted a cigarette, mused for a while and then stretched out on the sofa.

ANOTHER TRAP

With the first puff, the round face of Jean emerged before his eyes, and after that the face of Martha and then of his mother. He began to feel suffocated— his throat and lips became dry. He rushed to open the window fully and to fetch a bottle of beer from the refrigerator. In a few minutes he emptied several bottles, but his lips were as dry as before. To change his thoughts, he stood beside the window looking outside, where emptiness and darkness prevailed. He remained there for hours, until he saw the first rays of the rising sun.

With the advent of the morning, he tried to keep his routine as normal as he could. For two days nothing unusual happened. On the third day, about eight o'clock in the morning, he heard the sound of footsteps. Preparing himself for any eventuality, he opened the door as someone knocked. A tall, middle-aged man, who introduced himself as Sergeant Baker, and his companion as Constable Williams, said,

"I want to talk to Mr. Jack Kenneth about Marjory."

"It was a sad incident. I read it in the newspaper."

"A waitress told us that she was with you until ten o'clock on Sunday night."

"I met Marjory at the Niles about a month ago, Sergeant Baker. After that we met three or four times. On Sunday night we left the Niles early and I drove her home."

"Where to?"

"To Adolphus Street."

"Was there any reason to leave the Niles early, when it closes at one o'clock?"

"Marjory told me she had to see someone at home."

"Did she tell you the name of the person?"

"She did, but I forgot. As a matter of fact she used to mention the names of a lot of people. I was not in the least interested in them. I think she said it was her cousin."

Sergeant Baker made a note of the information Jack gave him, and left with the constable, saying "thanks."

The fear of something unknown was racking Jack's nerves, though he looked cool and composed. A waitress at the Niles knew he was a medical salesman. When he was at City Drug Store on one of his business trips, this waitress had come there to buy something. She had recognized him as a recent visitor to the Niles. She said "hello" and then asked if he worked at the same store. It was certain, he thought, that Marjory had told someone at home or at her office that she frequented the Niles on weekends. From there the sergeant must have gone to the Niles, where he showed Marjory's picture to all the employees, and this particular girl must have told him she had seen Marjory with me. The next step was easy— contact the manager of the drug store to find out the name and address of a handsome medical salesman, in his early thirties. The story appeared to be as simple as that. However, he wanted to forget these speculations for a while. He went to the bathroom for a quick shower, then left his apartment carrying his brief case.

Jack couldn't do much business, because he felt mentally fatigued the whole day. Somehow, he kept himself occupied. At about five o'clock when he returned, he saw two policemen waiting for him outside his apartment. His heart began to beat fast. One of them told him that Sergeant Baker wanted to see him at his office for further interrogation. Without offering any resistence, he accompanied them in the police car.

It was dusk when the car stopped in front of an iron gate. They entered a hall where Sergeant Baker was waiting for them. Smiling, he said,

"Mr. Kenneth, you told me this morning that from the Niles you drove Marjory back her apartment at Adolphus. Her parents told us that two days before her death, Marjory had left her apartment to stay with them. Perhaps Marjory forgot to tell you about it."

Controlling his emotions Jack said, "What difference does it make?"

"According to her parents she left home at eight o'clock in the evening, and after that they never saw her again. Of course you left the Niles at ten o'clock. From there, both of you went to the Rideau Canal. I want to hear the rest of the story from you. "

Jack grew pale. Softly he said, "There I strangled her. "

"And those teeth bites !"

"Those were mine. "

"Why did you do that?"

Jack was very humble in his answers. He struggled to explain, but the words stuck in his throat. Every attempt Sergeant Baker made to extract more information from Jack failed.

The story, with Jack's picture, appeared in the newspapers the next day. Lily was posing as a model when she saw Jack's picture. She looked at it for a few seconds and then read the account of the murder. "I think he's the same man," she shouted.

The artist was surprised at her outburst. Lily took the newspaper to show him. "I know him," she said. I think I must inform the police. "

"He has already confessed his crime !"

"There is something else to tell ... " She rushed to the telephone and dialed the police station. "May I talk to the man in charge of the Marjory murder case ?"

"One moment, please. "

In a few seconds she heard, "Sergeant Baker speaking. "

"This is Lily Brian. Six months ago I was working as a model in Toronto, where I met Jack Kenneth. He was the second male model

ANOTHER TRAP

and a very prominent one around the area. Many female models were jealous of his growing popularity. What I want to say is this ... two women were murdered then at a women's residence, in the same way that Marjory was killed. Those women were tall like Marjory, and nothing was missing from their apartments either !"

Sergeant Baker thanked her, noting her name and address. He got in touch with the Police Investigation Bureau of Toronto. The bureau confirmed Lily's report. Consequently, Jack was taken to Toronto. He confessed his crime, including the previous ones. The court sentenced him to life imprisonment.

The authorities were puzzled that in spite of strict surveillance he could have entered the women's residence. Jack solved the mystery by telling them he had used women's dresses and make-up, and that all the victims had been his friends. Concerning his motives for the murders, he still remained silent. However, he made a fervent appeal to officials that he be sent to a prison which was out of reach of his mother, and that she never be allowed to visit him.

DEATH OF A DREAM

Tomorrow would bring in its lap joys to your door. Guests would come to wish you a happy and long married life; here, in my bosom, aspirations will breathe their last. In a bride's gown you will be welcoming the visitors; whereas in a repentant's robe I will be entertaining my tears — the consorts of my loneliness. You will be lighting cigarettes, one after the other, and I will be whining, lying in a corner like a burnt-end thrown from your lips. What a difference! For the first time I am beginning to feel a vacuum — something lacking in life. I wish my parents had never sent me to college, in the hope of making me a lawyer.

Was it sheer coincidence or our fate? I cannot hit upon the right word— God knows why it was that I came to study at the same college where you entered, as a butterfly would a garden. For me it was a big leap from a school's simplicity to a college's modernity. Everyone

DEATH OF A DREAM

looked distant and alien to me. Books, as ever, were companions of my solitude. There were many for whom college was a resort for recreation. Some sought love as divers seek pearls — some sought to quench the thirst for knowledge. All of them were pilgrims of different shrines. On they marched, leaving behind the dust of their feet. You were in one of these groups. Time brought you nearer to me, first as a friend, later, as axis of my existence. I was a fount of clean and sweet water, covered with leaves. Spring was beginning to stretch itself. At such a point, you greeted me in the guise of a guide.

I had often seen you in the college library, poring over books— and exchanging notes. You never disturbed me till the day you sat across the table from me, wearing your favourite pink dress. Beams decked your round face frequently, as you read a volume of Byron's poetry. These beams made the tiny scar slightly above the right side of your lip clearly visible. The radiance of this intermittent rainbow captured my attention— it was a sort of hide and seek which I loved to watch with a squint. Slowly, you lifted your eyes from the book to ask me the time. I extended my left arm, enabling you to see the watch. You held my wrist— it lit a spark in me. You smiled— thanked— and left, looking curiously at me.

From that day on, my eyes searched for you

everywhere. The second day I saw you in the cafeteria. During the lunch hour, it was crowded as usual. Holding snacks in a tray, I glanced around to find a convenient place. You raised your hand from a corner of the room to indicate that the chair next to you was vacant. How much we talked that afternoon ! Boys and girls— some alone, others in company— passed by expressing their feelings through gestures. Some looked jealous— some envious— to many we appeared odd. Oblivious of them all, we kept talking for hours. When I left, I sensed the strings of life vibrating within me, producing a melody which enveloped my whole being. For me a celestial sun had emerged to bathe me in its rays— holy and pure.

After that it became almost a necessity for us to meet regularly. As a result, I went home late, got up late in the morning, often missed lectures. My target began to waver. At the end of the year I lost the scholarship, because I failed in the examination.

Your future is a ready-made garment— all you have to do is wear it. Being a banker's daughter you don't have to struggle, unlike a farmer's son. This is a huge gulf which I tried to cross. Dear Gloria, life is getting ashamed of me— it is reluctant to hold me dearly as it used to. Life gives birth to love, and love to memories. These memories are shaped into stories, from which leaps life. It's a good joke played upon mankind by a power divine.

You lighted the candle, I melted with its heat and flowed as a flood. As I neared the goal, you extinguished the light. In the dark, you disappeared as moths do. I cried and cried, standing alone amidst youth's wilderness, but you never came. It's more than a month, and still from you flows a current of memories which drives me to the racking sea. As a straw, which in spite of the slaps of mighty waves does not want to sink, I like to keep the memories alive. I know, one day, this straw would dash against the rock of death. When the tempests surround a person, hiding the warmth of the sun, these memories, however horrible and crude they may be, lull him. Moments create wounds, reminiscences scratch them, and time applies the balm. Today another stitch from the wound has broken. I wish all of them to break tonight so that I may shed tears of blood. You were right when you said, "cuts of love are second to none in sustaining pleasure." I will continue embracing the cuts as long as I can, though the sting of infidelity is beyond endurance.

Before going to your nuptial bed, think of the day when you took my hands, pressed them gently against your cheeks, then to your heart—caressed them like one deeply attached. Reflect how you used to call me "good", "intelligent", and "worthy of a woman's love." Often you pretended to read my palms, just to sit on my lap—

this used to impel me to kiss you till we were pushed onward by some force unknown to ecstacies inexpressible. Remember the words I often said, "If I were a poet, I would have caught your beauty in my creations; if I were a songster, I would have sung our love; if I were a sculptor, I would have immortalized your lovely form; if I were a painter, I would have drawn a portrait of your charm. Alas! I am nothing— simply an ardent votary of yours." You used to sob and sigh after hearing them. Tell me if it is possible for any mortal to relegate these episodes from the mind's treasury!

I had thought that love is God— it illuminates even the darkest corners— it is selfless— life without it is empty, futile and vain. In life's laboratory this proved wrong. It's difficult for me to believe that love is kind and it does not look for its interests. My friend was right who once said, "love is a mirage— a phantasmagoria of human mind. Parents seek their protection in their children, and lovers seek sexual satisfaction." He dubbed love as deception. How near the truth he was!

Our love has turned out to be ephemeral, like the span of the flowers which bloom in the morning and fade even before it is evening. It seems only a dream when I think of the days we passed together. Now I realize that love is an infant who is enticed by the glow of fire, not knowing there is heat in it which can burn his

DEATH OF A DREAM

hands; it is a rose with a bee hidden, which bites whosoever smells it; it is a well in a desert, which attracts tired and thirsty travellers who do not know of its dryness; it is hard like metal and callous like a stone.

The clock just struck three. This is not the first time sleep has become annoyed with me — the past has been constantly chasing me, as my shadow does. I can listen to the autumn creeping stealthily into my orchard. On the screen of night I view your eyes, which once conveyed a message to me; your lips which I loved to have so near; the rise of your youth which was mine. Within a few hours, someone else will come to drink from them. Before offering the vineyard, think — from there once flowed a spring to that distant valley which no longer is visible, on account of the thick fog gathered around it.

THE ETERNAL MYSTERY

"Ha! Ha! Ha!" Frank laughed and the dispersed empty beer bottles seemed to join him in his laughter. After sluggishly sipping beer from a glass he continued :

"I have looked into woman— woman who is the spirit of Mary— grace of the universe and the beauty of life. Woman who is a mother, a sister and also— a prostitute. You have seen women of different races— pretty, old, young, spinsters and widows. Alas! you don't know them. Have you seen Jean, the wife of that old professor of philosophy? I met her in the park, over there, near that canal, a month ago. She was sitting alone on a bench, looking at the setting sun. She was far from her surroundings. Fragments of white clouds, trailing and chasing one another along the horizon, had enraptured her. Slowly she moved her eyes from the dis-

tant objects to look for something in her wallet.
This was the time when she first looked at me
and I at her. There was a thirst in her eyes.
After saying hello, I sat beside her. During
our conversation she said, 'I do not like to talk
about pains, operations and sickness. Also, I
hate to discuss politics, current fashions, in-
flation, wars and the problems of families.' It
sounded to me as though she had memorized the
list. I found her to be an interesting person.
I did not know what to say when she asked me,
'What do you think of my likes ?'

"Noticing that I had no specific answer to
offer, she said, 'Think it over and let me know
tomorrow at the same place, same time.'

"The next day I met her with definite plans
in my mind. I had not made an effort to win her
over. We heard each other's heart throbbing
during the daytime, and even under the cover of
night. One thing that was beyond my compre-
hension was her attitude towards her husband.
All that I could gather from her was that he was
a professor who delivered long lectures, and
loved to explore the sea of knowledge contained
in bulky books.

"Time kept rolling on, and with time, our
relationship. But"— Frank resumed his talk
after taking a deep breath, "It's over a week
since she left me. I know that she will never
come back. She has found another friend— a
better one."

THE ETERNAL MYSTERY

Frank became quiet, and stared out the window, where he could see snowflakes falling silently over the solitary streets, and the lonely lamp-posts emitting their dim lights. A few yards away, some melancholy figures treaded cautiously. To the left, two bare trees, spotted with patches of snow here and there, appeared to be shedding tears. Frank glanced at them. Taking a glass in his hand, he spoke again,

"Alex, besides many, I loved Patricia— a telephone operator, who aspired to be a heroine of the film industry. And ..."

"Stop this nonsense." Alex exclaimed. Drop it. I don't want to hear more. Love is not contemptible, Frank, nor is woman, whom you think of as an instrument for gratification of your lust. If woman is a heart, love is its palpitation. She too was a woman who brought you into this world. Love is not smutty, as your thoughts are. It is that spark that illuminates the darkest corners of man's life. Your love is a sexual passion, a temporary need of the time. You expect from a woman only her body."

"Love can never be smutty, I thought the same," Frank replied. "In life's arena, it proved absolutely wrong. I'll tell you of an incident that changed my life. I don't know when I lost my mother. My father was the pillar of my hopes and aspirations. He died when I was studying for my B. A. After his death, I had to quit college to earn my living. To console my-

90

self I sought refuge in the outer world. One day, when I was thinking about my past and future, sitting with a cup of coffee in a restaurant, I heard a familiar voice. When I turned round I saw Martha standing before me. We had passed our school-leaving examination at the same school. She asked me about my work, marriage, parents, and many other things in almost a single breath. Her straightforward and fearless approach amazed me. At school she was regarded as a model of shyness and modesty. Time had changed her strikingly. After a few minutes' casual talk, she left me with an invitation for tea the following day.

"After that we met regularly. Our relationship matured with each successive day. I began considering her as the centre of my being. Alex, there was something in her that bothered me. I had often seen her with other men. Whenever I asked her about them, she would smile first, and then say, 'I think that you have grown suspicious.' Her usual answer was, 'He was my cousin.' She would kiss me after saying so.

"What do you think of me?" Martha often asked.

"A charming creation of Nature— a moon— nay— essence of my life."

"No, not in the least." Soon her eyes would become tearful. With a heavy voice she would say, "I don't believe it."

"I can't forget the day I received my salary;

it was the second month of our romance. After the soul-destroying work at the office, I went straight to her. I told Martha I had my salary in my pocket and that I wanted to buy her a present. She was sad and contemplative. Her tired blue eyes began to shine as she heard these words. With a leap she embraced me warmly a couple of times. Loosening her hold, she said, "Frank, I have received my gift."

"No, I want to give you another gift," I persisted.

"My mother is seriously ill. I have to go home early today to get her medicine." Without waiting for my reply, she stepped towards the door.

"For a long time I kept wondering at her behaviour. At the same time, I was tortured with a desire to see her soon. I began to muse on the pleasures of the next day. Thoughts came up like bubbles, random and aimless. I pictured her standing close to me, repeating the words she had uttered before leaving. As my thoughts were hovering like butterflies over the flowers of delight, I slipped my hands into my pockets. My wallet was missing."

After a long pause, Frank spoke, "Don't you think that is what a woman is ? This shocking incident brought me nearer the truth. One evening I saw her again. She was with a man in one of the rooms of a hotel. I saw her coming out of the room like a tired hunter. Her breath smelled of whiskey. She held a purse in one of her hands. I looked at her, but she, without taking notice of me went away in the man's blue Buick. "

Frank stood up with a jerk, lighted his cigarette, and strode towards the refrigerator. Alex, who had been silent, was driven to analyze Frank in the light of his experiences. Mentally he prepared himself to interrogate him. Before he could open his mouth, Frank came back with a fresh bottle of beer and said, "Can you guess who that man was ?" Without waiting, Frank himself provided the answer, "My boss— my boss, for whom autumn is a notion. His interest in wine and women is proverbial, though he is a husband and the father of three children. His neat and well-tailored clothes and dyed hair conceal the fifty-five springs he has seen.

"When I arrived at the office next morning, one of my colleagues told me that the boss wanted me in his office. This alarmed me; I didn't know what to expect. I began to think of replies to his possible queries. Soon I mustered my courage and quietly entered his office. He smiled, looked at me, while pointing towards the chair in front of him. He asked politely, again with a smile, 'So you know Martha ?'

"I didn't know whether his smile was derisive, or friendly. Before admitting anything, I had to understand his motives. Being cautious,

THE ETERNAL MYSTERY

I preferred to be general and laconic, 'She was once my class-fellow.' I, too, tried to smile this time.

" 'Listen,' the boss spoke. 'I have no right to invade your privacy. Somehow, I got interested in her. She, presumably, is too proud to reveal her life's scar to anyone. I've come to know from some scattered sources that she has a bedridden mother and a sister attending school, whose support she has taken upon herself. Her father died of heavy drinking when she was still a young girl. But'— he hesitated a little at this point to complete the sentence— 'she offers what you pay for'. Smilingly, he took a file and said, 'I hope you will give me more information about her. Please come another time for more talks.' "

A CONTEMPORARY POET

"Doctor !" Tom Murphy cried in a soft and feeble voice— but no one was there. The doctor had left. The cold of January was penetrating, though the heater was fully on. He wrapped both the blankets tightly around himself. While doing so, he glanced at the picture of Gloria lying on the table. He heaved a deep sigh, and then began to gaze at the picture as if it were new to him. Within a few minutes, he pushed the curtains aside to have a better view of the exterior world. Night was beginning to fall. He began to think of the past.

Once again, he was at his university, where he was considered the best poet of the city. His fame and handsomeness brought many girls into his life. None of them could claim his undivided attention. Gloria's arrival was like a breath of spring which put new life into him.

Gloria was a worker for pacifism, and as such it was her ambition to see a world government established. Her devotion to the cause, and the confidence she reflected through her speech and manners, made Tom Murphy her admirer. He was a poet of wine and women and youth. He could express himself in a charming and rhythmical language. Many of his verses were about the women he knew. Gloria had become the centre of his poetic creations since he met her. It made Gloria happy— though she ardently desired to see him using his pen to make people and nations aware of the great threats to peace— armament and nuclear weapons. This had nothing to do with the artistic creed of Tom Murphy. He was of the opinion that a poet has no obligations to society. He has his own world— he writes to please himself and others, not to preach. He feared that no one would buy poetry that is concentrated on politics. Besides, girls would not be interested in his art if it did not concern them.

On his birthday, he gave a small party for his friends. Drinks and dinner were followed by poetry reading. His audience was spellbound by the magic of the masculinity of his voice, and the vivid words he used in his poetry. Gloria was sad and serious amidst this lively group. When all the guests had departed, Tom Murphy opened the gifts he had received from them. There were translations of Charles Baudelaire, and Omar Khayyam, a volume of Byron, paintings of nude women, bottles of perfumes and shave lotions. Gloria's box contained two books entitled 'The War That Will End War', and 'A Question of Survival'. He turned some of the pages at random. There was a small note addressed to him, "I'm leaving early in the morning for Amsterdam for two years to study further the problem of international peace. It is my wish that you read these books, so that I may find you a different person when I return."

Days changed into weeks, and weeks into months. It did not take long for Tom Murphy to stifle the pangs of separation. Time helped in healing the wound, which he buried in pursuit of his usual preoccupations. During this period, he was suddenly taken ill. Doctors diagnosed it as a weakening of the heart and the kidneys. Gradually, his condition began to deteriorate.

Outside, the moon was covering every visible object with its silvery beams. He shuddered— a premonition of something unknown began to invade him. He drew the curtain back over the window, stood up, and looked at the calendar hanging on the wall. In a few hours, he thought, it will be dawn. He mused for a while— suddenly picked up the books which Gloria had given him. He turned a few pages— went through the underlined passages with the notes he had scribbled at the margin, then collected a heap of papers he had kept under those books. It gave him relief to read them, inserting corrections here and there.

A CONTEMPORARY POET

Night's darkness was dissolving. He was cold and sleepy— for many a night he had not slept. He wished to go to sleep in the morning. When the clock strikes six, he would be in the thirty-sixth year of his life. At that hour, he would like to depart quietly, unlike his arrival in this world. A child's cry is considered to be a sign of life, and therefore, he is made to cry if he doesn't. This lays the cornerstone of his future. As he grows old he tries to escape it, though unconsciously, with the help of multicoloured toys which remain his lifelong companions. As an orator, he plays with the sentiments of the masses; as a patriot, he sows seeds of hatred; as a scientist, he invents toys of destruction; as a politician, he plays with the bloodbath of innocent citizens. He began to visualize toys in different shapes and sizes— from a child's pacifier and balloon to huge tanks, bombers, cannons, machine guns, and anti-ballistic missiles. While so thinking, he wearied, his eyes began to close. He perceived a new light— his steps proceeded towards it.

In the morning, Gloria came to see him. Close to him were lying the books she gave him two years ago. Underneath, there was a bundle of papers. She skimmed through them in a great hurry; these were poems to denounce war, armament, pollution, racial discrimination, and on many more subjects concerning international cooperation. The one she liked most

A CONTEMPORARY POET

was about One World Government. She looked at the poet— he was asleep, like a child. A flood arose from her eyes. She knelt down and gently embraced his cold body.

ALSO BY STEPHEN GILL :

Stephen Gill is also a poet. His poetry is concise in form and universal in application. His themes are commonplace and the contemporary social concerns, which place his poetry in the eternal as well as in the here and now. He does not wish to shock or impress his reader. His purpose is to suggest, to hint, to impart with grace.

REFLECTIONS(a collection of poems)
48 pages, soft, price $1. 75

WOUNDS(a collection of poems)
44 pages, soft, price $ 2. 50

A FEW COMMENTS

About REFLECTIONS(a collection of poems) by
Stephen Gill :

THE DAILY STANDARD-FREEHOLDER
"These poems run the gamut from childhood to
youth to maturity, dealing with the human condition in simple but beautiful language... The
poems in this book are worth reading." (Russ
Dewar, Managing Editor, The Standard-Freeholder)

THE CANADIAN INDIA TIMES
"In his first volume of poetry Stephen Gill ex-
presses this same timely and significant theme
of world unity. But there is variety of theme
and tone in these twenty four poems. He writes
of childhood, youth, maturity and love. Most
poems, however, contain at their core the need
for love between persons and nations... There
is, in Mr. Gill's mature work, a public despair
but private hope. Survival and growth of the
person and the nation begins with inner enlight-
ment, inner awareness of the principle of survival— Love.
"But there is in Tennyson's poem and Mr. Gill's
volume a hierarchy of values." (Dr. Frank M.
Tierney, Professor of English, University of
Ottawa)

(Continued on next page...)

SARNIA OBSERVER
"He (Stephen Gill) is most certainly a world citizen in his choice of themes, for searching, suffering, looking back, and loving are conditions common to all mankind... From the world in cupped hands, cover design, to the last page of the book, there is a plea for universal peace... Poets such as Stephen Gill are certainly doing their utmost to promote such world unity. " (Norma West Linder)

HARBINGER
"This collection of poems leaves the reader with a message of love which is perhaps its greatest message. " (Jack McLean)

QUILL & QUIRE
"They strive to become Jocean 'epiphanies', leading the reader through an examination of the insignificant and the commonplace to an awareness of the concerns of larger human society..." (Garth Turner)

PREFACE
"Mr. Gill's poems are concise. No tedious belaboring of non-essential mars their precision. They are capsuled feelings and meanings, dross stripped experience speaking for itself in an era of similar experiences, but unique in the personality and expression of their author. They are good poems. " (Dr. Richard N. Pollard, Professor of English, University of Ottawa)

Date Due

APR 8 8 1987			